SUPERKID
SCIENCE QUIZ

Dilip M. Salwi is a Delhi-based science writer. A winner of several national awards and fellowships for popularizing science, he also writes science fiction and plays involving science and scientists. Author of forty-four books, his *The Robots are Coming, 1000 Science Quiz, Meet the Four Elements, The Story of Zero, Chemline Book of Quotable Science, Folk Tales of Science* and *Inventions that Made History* are bestsellers.

SUPERKID

SCIENCE QUIZ

(For 6 to 10 year-olds)

Dilip M. Salwi

RUPA

Published by
Rupa Publications India Pvt. Ltd 2002
7/16, Ansari Road, Daryaganj
New Delhi 110002

Sales centres:

Allahabad Bengaluru Chennai
Hyderabad Jaipur Kathmandu
Kolkata Mumbai

ISBN: 978-81-716-7659-0

Eight impression 2019

10 9 8

The moral right of the author has been asserted.

To
my nephew
Ajinkya Salvi
who would love to have this quiz book

Welcome, Young Quiz buffs!

Quiz culture has come to India. Thanks to TV serials like Amitabh Bachhan's *Kaun Banega Crorepati* and its clones, a quiz craze has been generated among children. The interest in quiz among the younger generation struck me particularly when I found my son as well as my nephew very keen to watch KBC as well as ready to quiz each other and answer questions. Later, on enquiries, I found the concept of quiz very popular among children at large. They quiz each other even in school buses, not to speak of classes and playground. Not surprisingly, a spate of quiz books has appeared in the market.

I took up the idea of writing a quiz book especially targeting the children when I was on a Fellowship in Munich, Germany. In fact, I started my work on the book in the International Youth Library there. But after returning home and several discussions with my wife Smriti, who is a primary school teacher, I felt the need for preparing two quiz books instead of the originally planned one since the levels of exposure and understanding of children of primary and secondary classes differ.

Taking into account various factors, such as, exposure, interest, knowledge, etc. I have planned the questions in such a manner that at least 60 per cent of the questions in this book are picked up from what is taught in his (or her) school; the rest are based on his (or her) observation, exposure and intelligence. Some questions have been purposely included in the book because as a modern child he should know their answers. In other words, the book would not only judge how good a child is at science but also improve his knowledge of general science.

I am sure this book will go a long way in arousing a child's interest in science. Happy quizzing!

National Science Day   Dilip M. Salwi
February 28, 2001

Acknowledgements

Thanks to my wife Smriti for the discussions I had with her while I was preparing this book. I also thank my son Romel for his suggestions and criticisms on the questions from time to time. Ajay Gupta has also to be thanked for keying in this book on computer.

Last but not the least I thank all my family members including my daughter Neha for bearing patiently with me while I was busy writing this book.

Dilip M. Salwi

Contents

I

LIFE AND LIVING BEINGS

Animals

1. Which family of animals does a zebra belong to?
   (a) Horse
   (b) Dog
   (c) Cat
   (d) Rat

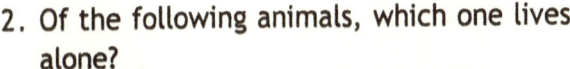

2. Of the following animals, which one lives alone?
   (a) Zebra   (b) Wildebeest
   (c) Wolf   (d) Tiger

3. Of the following animals, which one is not found in the polar regions?
   (a) Reindeer   (b) Fox
   (c) Seal   (d) Lizard

4. Of the following animals, which one has a pouch to carry its young?
   (a) Gorilla   (b) Hare
   (c) Kangaroo   (d) Deer

5. Of the following animals, which one lays eggs?
   (a) Snake   (b) Cow
   (c) Elephant   (d) Dog

6. Which family of animals does a tiger belong to?
   (a) Dog
   (b) Cat
   (c) Rat
   (d) Deer

7. Which animal has a pair of visible, big teeth which are not meant for eating? *
   (a) Elephant   (b) Crocodile
   (c) Tiger   (d) Nilgai

8. Of the following animals, which one tries to save itself by merging with the surroundings?
   (a) Kangaroo
   (b) Zebra
   (c) Rhinoceros
   (d) Wild boar

9. Of the following animals, which one is cold-blooded?
   (a) Crocodile   (b) Mongoose
   (c) Fox   (d) Monkey

10. Of the following animals, which one is not kept in a zoo?
    (a) Jackal   (b) Wolf
    (c) Hyena   (d) Dog

11. Of the following animals, which one lives in holes in the ground?
    (a) Monkey   (b) Tiger
    (c) Rabbit   (d) Frog

12. Which family of animals does a wolf belong to?
    (a) Dog
    (b) Cat
    (c) Deer
    (d) Rat

13. Of the following animals, which one is warm-blooded?
    (a) Snake   (b) Frog
    (c) Salamander   (d) Hippopotamus

14. Of the following animals, which one is adopted as a pet?
    (a) Rabbit   (b) Crocodile
    (c) Hyena   (d) Wolf

15. Of the following animals, which one hunts in packs?
    (a) Cheetah   (b) Lion
    (c) Tiger   (d) Leopard

16. Of the following animals, which one lives on trees?
    - (a) Squirrel
    - (b) Rat
    - (c) Deer
    - (d) Jackal

17. Of the following animals, which two chew cud?
    - (a) Buffalo
    - (b) Cow
    - (c) Rabbit
    - (d) Cat

18. Which class of animals can live both on land and in water?
    - (a) Amphibian
    - (b) Reptile
    - (c) Dinosaur
    - (d) All

19. Of the following animals, which one is useful to us?
    - (a) Rhinoceros
    - (b) Giraffe
    - (c) Panther
    - (d) Camel

20. Of the following animals, which one eats both animals and plants?
    - (a) Lion
    - (b) Bear
    - (c) Monkey
    - (d) Fox

21. From which animal is wool taken?
    - (a) Horse
    - (b) Sheep
    - (c) Cow
    - (d) Snake

22. Of the following animals, which one is a plant eater?
    - (a) Rhinoceros
    - (b) Racoon
    - (c) Bear
    - (d) Hyena

23. Of the following animals, which one lays eggs in water?
    (a) Python   (b) Frog
    (c) Cow   (d) Crocodile

24. Of the following animals, which one is wild?
    (a) Donkey   (b) Lion
    (c) Goat   (d) Horse

25. What is a tiger hunted for?
    (a) Skin   (b) Nail
    (c) Bones   (d) All

26. Of the following animals, which one has a pair of horns?
    (a) Antelope   (b) Elephant
    (c) Zebra   (d) Fox

27. Which animal has one horn?
    (a) Rhinoceros   (b) Bison
    (c) Antelope   (d) Cow

28. Which is the national animal of India?
    (a) Lion   (b) Elephant
    (c) Tiger   (d) Fox

29. What is an elephant hunted for?
    (a) Skin
    (b) Hair
    (c) Teeth
    (d) Ears

30. Of the following animals, which one lives on a tree?
    (a) Kangaroo   (b) Monkey
    (c) Giraffe   (d) Rabbit

Birds

31. Of the following birds, which one has liking for the food that man eats and is therefore always around houses?
    (a) Crow   (b) Hoopoe
    (c) Woodpecker   (d) Tailor bird

32. Of the following birds, which one can see in the night?
    (a) Great horned owl
    (b) House sparrow
    (c) Crow pheasant
    (d) Pigeon

33. Of the following birds, which one dives into water to catch fishes?
    (a) Hornbill   (b) Kingfisher
    (c) Owl   (d) Gannet

34. Which bird is a symbol of peace?
    (a) Pigeon   (b) Dove
    (c) Peacock   (d) Sparrow

35. Of the following birds, which one eats fish?
    (a) Ostrich   (b) Swallow
    (c) Pelican   (d) Parrot

36. Of the following birds, which one preys on another bird?
    (a) Falcon   (b) Heron
    (c) Starling   (d) Cockatoo

37. Of the following birds, which one does not fly?
    (a) Emu   (b) Ibis
    (c) Gannet   (d) Cormorant

38. Of the following birds, which one has a sharp and curved beak?
    (a) Stork   (b) Pigeon
    (c) Hoopoe   (d) Eagle

39. Of the following birds, which one has a long and pointed beak?
    (a) Parrot   (b) Sparrow
    (c) Stork   (d) Crow

40. Which bird is always found in a group of seven and makes much noise?
    (a) Parrot
    (b) Blue magpie
    (c) Common babbler
    (d) Common crow

41. Of the following birds, which one has webbed feet?
    (a) Duck   (b) Egret
    (c) Stork   (d) Pigeon

42. Of the following birds, which one eats worms found in the ground?
    (a) Hoopoe   (b) Parakeet
    (c) Penguin   (d) Albatross

43. Of the following birds, which one eats rats?
    (a) Spoonbill   (b) Pintail duck
    (c) Tailor bird   (d) Owl

44. Of the following birds, which one wades through water?
    (a) Egret   (b) Swan
    (c) Weaver bird   (d) All

45. Which bird has a crest on its head that it opens and shuts like a fan?
    (a) Hoopoe
    (b) Racket-tailed drongo
    (c) Golden oriole
    (d) Woodpecker

46. Of the following birds, which one is not kept in a zoo?
    (a) Munia   (b) Bulbul
    (c) Sparrow   (d) Flamingo

47. Of the following birds, which one sucks nectar from flowers?
    (a) Heron   (b) Sunbird
    (c) Parrot   (d) Swan

48. Of the following birds, which one eats both flesh and grains?
    (a) Crow   (b) Owl
    (c) Eagle   (d) Sparrow

49. Which bird, though known for melodious singing, lays her eggs in a crow's nest?
    (a) Flamingo
    (b) Koel
    (c) Racket-tailed drongo
    (d) Grey heron

50. Of the following birds, which one changes its home seasonally?
    (a) Sunbird
    (b) Siberian crane
    (c) Pigeon
    (d) Green bee-eater

51. Of the following birds, which one climbs on trees?
    (a) Wagtail
    (b) Woodpecker
    (c) Quail
    (d) Lark

52. Of the following birds, which ones imitate the sounds they hear?
    (a) Crane   (b) Myna
    (c) Pigeon   (d) Parrot

53. Of the following birds, which one is seen in coastal areas?
   (a) Puffin
   (b) Skylark
   (c) Robin
   (d) Babbler

54. Which bird looks like a sparrow except during mating season?
   (a) Common kingfisher
   (b) Tree pie
   (c) Weaver bird
   (d) Black ibis

55. Which is the national bird of India?
   (a) Flamingo
   (b) Peacock
   (c) Parrot
   (d) Sarus crane

56. Of the following birds, which one is often seen in pairs?
   (a) Sarus crane
   (b) Flamingo
   (c) Parrot
   (d) Blue magpie

Other Living Beings

57. Which living beings are called "Little ploughmen"?
   (a) Snail
   (b) Earthworm
   (c) Snake
   (d) All

58. Of the following living beings, which one cannot hear sounds?
    (a) Lobster   (b) Scorpion
    (c) Snake   (d) Spider

59. Which living being eats up and destroys plants and fields?
    (a) Locust   (b) Weevil
    (c) Caterpillar   (d) All

60. Of the following living beings, which one attacks its enemies with poison?
    (a) Crab   (b) Cobra
    (c) Shark   (d) Whale

61. Which living being is often found in books and papers?
    (a) Cockroach   (b) Silverfish
    (c) Cricket   (d) Bedbug

62. Which living being is found in human hair?
    (a) Lice
    (b) Cockroach
    (c) Flea
    (d) Spider

63. Of the following living beings, which one can fly?
    (a) Mosquito
    (b) Butterfly
    (c) Locust
    (d) All

64. Of the following living beings, which one makes its home in beds, pillows and sheets?
    (a) Bug   (b) Mosquito
    (c) Housefly   (d) Butterfly

65. Of the following living beings, which one has no legs?
    (a) Fish   (b) Caterpillar
    (c) Honey bee   (d) Lobster

66. Of the following living beings, which one can break and grow its own tail quickly?
    (a) Spider   (b) Cockroach
    (c) Lizard   (d) Caterpillar

67. Of the following living beings, which one eats insects?
    (a) Gecko   (b) Frog
    (c) Spider   (d) All

68. Of the following living beings, which one is found in a desert?
    (a) Scorpion   (b) Cactus
    (c) Red ant   (d) All

69. Of the following living beings, which one lives in colonies?
    (a) Cockroach
    (b) Ant
    (c) Snail
    (d) Millipede

70. Of the following living beings, which one forms swarms?
(a) Honeybee   (b) Ladybird
(c) Dragonfly   (d) Grasshopper

71. Of the following living beings, which one weaves webs to catch its prey?
(a) Butterfly
(b) Ladybird
(c) Spider
(d) Ant

72. Of the following living beings, which one does not have tentacles?
(a) Starfish   (b) Octopus
(c) Whelk   (d) Jellyfish

73. What do earthworms use to breathe in air?
(a) Skin   (b) Lung
(c) Gills   (d) Tubes

74. Of the following living beings, which one does not have a hard covering?
(a) Lobster   (b) Eel
(c) Crayfish   (d) Crab

75. Of the following living beings, which one cannot fly?
(a) Grasshopper   (b) Housefly
(c) Butterfly   (d) Mosquito

76. Of the following living beings, which ones carry their home along with them?
    (a) Snail   (b) Spider
    (c) Tortoise   (d) Beetle

77. Of the following living beings, which one has several legs?
    (a) Spider   (b) Cockroach
    (c) Slug   (d) Centipede

78. Of the following living beings, which one swallows its prey?
    (a) Cobra   (b) Crab
    (c) Python   (d) Beetle

79. Of the following living beings, which one has feet shaped like paddles?
    (a) Turtle   (b) Crocodile
    (c) Eel   (d) None

80. Of the following living beings, which one has legs?
    (a) Seahorse   (b) Snail
    (c) Cockroach   (d) Python

81. Of the following living beings, which one has fins?
    (a) Octopus
    (b) Shark
    (c) Tortoise
    (d) Crab

Life

82. What does a seed need to grow into a plant?
    (a) Fertile soil   (b) Sunlight
    (c) Water   (d) All

83. When cow dung, human and plant waste are allowed to rot, what do they produce?
    (a) Manure   (b) Loam
    (c) Soil   (d) Rock

84. What is a 'baby' frog called?
    (a) Tadpole
    (b) Puppy
    (c) Kitten
    (d) Pony

85. What is a flesh-eating animal called?
    (a) Herbivore
    (b) Carnivore
    (c) Omnivore
    (d) None

86. What is the shape of a cell in a beehive?
    (a) Triangle   (b) Square
    (c) Hexagon   (d) Circle

87. How many legs do insects have?
    (a) Two   (b) Four
    (c) Six   (d) Eight

88. What spreads seeds from one place to another?
    (a) Wind   (b) Water
    (c) Living beings (d) All

89. Of the following living beings, which one has no bone?
    (a) Snake   (b) Gecko
    (c) Crab   (d) Giraffe

90. Where are annual rings produced in a tree?
    (a) Trunk   (b) Branches
    (c) Leaves   (d) Flowers

91. What is needed to make soil healthy for the growth of plants?
    (a) Pesticide   (b) Insecticide
    (c) Fertilizer   (d) Cow dung

92. What is the basic unit in all living beings?
    (a) Blood   (b) Cell
    (c) Protein   (d) None

93. What fixes plants and trees firmly into the soil?
    (a) Branches   (b) Stem
    (c) Leaves   (d) Roots

94. Where do earthworms live?
    (a) Soil
    (b) Water
    (c) Air
    (d) Vacuum

95. What do plants and trees breathe through?
    (a) Leaves   (b) Trunk
    (c) Roots   (d) All

96. Of the following living beings, which one has no bone?
    (a) Shark   (b) Crocodile
    (c) Octopus   (d) Cow

97. Which organ do fishes use to breathe in air?
    (a) Tubes   (b) Gills
    (c) Skin   (d) Lungs

98. What produces food?
    (a) Sunlight   (b) Plants
    (c) Water   (d) All

99. What takes food for the plant from the ground?
    (a) Stem   (b) Leaves
    (c) Roots   (d) Flowers

100. Which living beings have compound eyes?
    (a) Birds   (b) Insects
    (c) Animals   (d) Fishes

101. Of the following living beings, which one has a backbone?
    (a) Oyster
    (b) Starfish
    (c) Salamander
    (d) Silverfish

102. Of the following living beings, which one lives both on land and water?
- (a) Mongoose
- (b) Frog
- (c) Mouse
- (d) Shrew

103. What is a plant-eating animal called?
- (a) Omnivore
- (b) Carnivore
- (c) Herbivore
- (d) All

II

HUMAN BODY AND FOOD

The Human Body

104. Of the following organs, which one does not take part in breathing?
     (a) Nose passages
     (b) Lungs
     (c) Trachea
     (d) Heart

105. Of the following parts of the human body, which one is a liquid?
     (a) Skeleton   (b) Blood
     (c) Brain   (d) Lung

106. How many muscles are required for smiling?
     (a) 40   (b) 26
     (c) 14   (c) 9

107. How do germs enter our bodies?
     (a) Through wounds
     (b) Through food
     (c) Through air
     (d) All

108. What communicates message in the human body?
    (a) Brain   (b) Nerves
    (c) Muscles   (d) All

109. How many types of teeth do we have?
    (a) Three   (b) Four
    (c) Five   (d) Six

110. Of the following parts of the human body, which one is present in the chest?
    (a) Heart   (b) Lung
    (c) Ribs   (d) All

111. Of the following parts of the human body, which one is not a bone?
    (a) Skull   (b) Rib
    (c) Intestine   (d) Jawbone

112. How many sense organs do we have?
    (a) Three   (b) Four
    (c) Five   (d) Six

113. What circulates oxygen to different parts of the human body?
    (a) Lung   (b) Vein
    (c) Blood   (d) Brain

114. What pumps blood to all the parts of the human body?
    (a) Lung   (b) Heart
    (c) Liver   (d) All

115. Of the following parts of the human body, which one is not an organ?
(a) Heart   (b) Skull
(c) Pancreas   (d) Stomach

116. Which organ of the human body is filled with air when it is breathed in?
(a) Lung   (b) Heart
(c) Liver   (d) Stomach

117. How many bones are present in the backbone of human beings?
(a) 30   (b) 31
(c) 32   (d) 33

118. Which organ of the human body is filled with food when it is eaten?
(a) Liver
(b) Stomach
(c) Pancreas
(d) Wind pipe

119. What carries blood from heart to different parts of the human body?
(a) Vein   (b) Artery
(c) Nerve   (d) Cartilage

120. Which is the waste produced by the human body?
(a) Sweat   (b) Urine
(c) Faeces   (d) All

121. Of the following things, which one is not a part of the nervous system?
    (a) Nerves   (b) Spinal cord
    (c) Brain   (d) Liver

122. How many teeth does an adult human being has?
    (a) 16   (b) 32
    (c) 44   (d) 52

Foods, Fruits, etc.

123. What is Ketchup made up of?
    (a) Tomato
    (b) Potato
    (c) Banana
    (d) Carrot

124. Of the following food items, which one is produced from plants?
    (a) Cheese   (b) Potatoes
    (c) Prawn   (d) Cream

125. Which fruit grows on a creeper?
    (a) Grapes   (b) Orange
    (c) Guava   (d) Mango

126. Of the following food items, which is a product of milk?
    (a) Corn flakes   (b) Peas
    (c) Eggs   (d) Yoghurt

127. Of the following seeds, which is crushed to give oil used for various purposes?
(a) Coconut   (b) Mustard
(c) Almond   (d) All

128. Of the following food items, which one is a spice?
(a) Pepper   (b) Maize
(c) Peas   (d) Barley

129. Of the following plants, whose leaves are cooked and eaten?
(a) Spinach   (b) Ginger
(c) Tomato   (d) Potato

130. Of the following food items, which one is not pulses?
(a) Rajmah   (b) Dal
(c) Beans   (d) Wheat

131. What is "Chapati" made of?
(a) Wheat   (b) Rice
(c) Corn   (d) Barley

132. Of the following food items, which one is not a nut?
(a) Cashewnut   (b) Almond
(c) Rice   (d) Walnut

133. Which fruit grows on a tree?
(a) Tomato   (b) Apple
(c) Peas   (d) Brinjal

134. Of the following food items, which one is not used as a vegetable?
(a) Potato　　　　(b) Orange
(c) Brinjal　　　　(d) Tomato

135. Of the following vegetables, which one grows under the ground?
(a) Potato　　　　(b) Carrot
(c) Ginger　　　　(d) All

136. Of the following food items, which one is eaten only after it is cooked?
(a) Spinach　　　　(b) Cabbage
(c) Tomato　　　　(d) Onion

137. Of the following plants, whose leaves are cooked and eaten?
(a) Brinjal　　　　(b) Banana
(c) Cabbage　　　　(d) Peas

138. Of the following food items, which one is used as a cooking oil?
(a) Ground nut　　(b) Coconut
(c) Mustard　　　　(d) All

139. Which fruit has only one seed?
(a) Water melon　(b) Mango
(c) Orange　　　　(d) Guava

24

140. Of the following food items, which one is eaten raw as salad?
(a) Potato   (b) Cabbage
(c) Brinjal   (d) Apple

141. What portion of its plant is 'coffee'?
(a) Dried leaves   (b) Dried roots
(c) Dried seeds   (d) Dried stems

142. Of the following food items, which one is not used for making jam?
(a) Pineapple   (b) Apple
(c) Peas   (d) Grapes

143. What portion of its plant is 'tea'?
(a) Dried seeds   (b) Dried leaves
(c) Dried roots   (d) Dried stems

144. Of the following food items, which is not the product of a plant?
(a) Cooking oil   (b) Bread
(c) Butter   (d) Carrot

III

DAILY LIFE, THINGS

Daily Life

145. Of the following sounds, which one is not natural?
    (a) Snoring of a sleeping person
    (b) Mewing of a cat
    (c) Honking of a car
    (d) Chirping of a bird

146. When are the shadows smallest?
    (a) At noon   (b) Morning
    (c) Evening   (d) All

147. When is the Moon generally seen in the sky?
    (a) Night   (b) Sunrise
    (c) Sunset   (d) All

148. Which gadget converts electricity into heat?
    (a) Room heater   (b) Iron
    (c) Geyser   (d) All

149. What most living things need to be alive?
    (a) Food   (b) Water
    (c) Air   (d) All

150. What mainly causes tides in the seas?
    (a) Moon   (b) Sun
    (c) Mars   (d) Comet

151. Which is the most commonly used substance in all walks of life?
    (a) Salt   (b) Petrol
    (c) Water   (d) Sugar

152. Of the following sounds, which one is natural?
    (a) Zooming of an aeroplane
    (b) Zug-zug of a train
    (c) Ticking of a clock
    (d) Soughing of winds

153. Which colour is formed when red is mixed with blue?
    (a) Pink   (b) Brown
    (c) Purple   (d) Green

154. What heats up water in a boiling pot?
    (a) Conduction   (b) Insulation
    (c) Convection   (d) Condensation

155. What is the shape of an egg?
    (a) Round
    (b) Oval
    (c) Square
    (d) Triangle

156. Which is the scale used for measuring temperature of the human body?
(a) Reaumer   (b) Fahrenheit
(c) Kelvin   (d) Centigrade

157. Which means of transport is shaped like a bird?
(a) Railway   (b) Bus
(c) Aeroplane   (d) Tram

158. What is a 'leap year'?
(a) 29 days in February
(b) 28 days in February
(c) 29 days in November
(d) 28 days in November

159. Which colour is formed when yellow and red are mixed?
(a) Blue   (b) Green
(c) Orange   (d) Pink

160. How many colours are present in a rainbow?
(a) Three   (b) Seven
(c) Five   (d) Four

161. Of the following sources of light, which one is natural?
(a) Neon sign   (b) Tubelight
(c) Firefly   (d) Electric bulb

162. Which rays are used for detecting a fracture in a human bone?
(a) Ultraviolet rays (b) X-rays
(c) Infrared rays   (d) All

Things

163. Of the following things, which one involves a chemical change?
    (a) Waxing Moon
    (b) Stretched rubber band
    (c) Burning paper
    (d) All

164. Of the following things, which one has a regular shape and size?
    (a) Brick   (b) Leaf
    (c) Feather   (d) Notebook

165. Of the following things, which one is sold by weight?
    (a) Milk   (b) Cold drink
    (c) Vegetable   (d) Coconut oil

166. Of the following things, which one does not dissolve in water?
    (a) Sand   (b) Common salt
    (c) Sugar   (d) All

167. Of the following things, which one is a rock?
    (a) Marble flooring
    (b) Coal seam
    (c) Grindstone
    (d) All

168. Of the following things, which one is a simple machine?
    (a) Wrench   (b) Knife
    (c) Crowbar   (d) All

169. Of the following things, which one has a shape?
    (a) Temperature   (b) Light
    (c) Pressure   (d) Area

170. Of the following things, which one is not a force?
    (a) Friction   (b) Gravity
    (c) Pressure   (d) Temperature

171. Of the following things, which one allows light to pass through it?
    (a) Paper   (b) Glass
    (c) Wood   (d) Iron

172. Of the following things, which one originally comes from an animal?
    (a) Coal   (b) Sand
    (c) Nylon   (d) All

173. Of the following things, which one has no colour?
    (a) Water
    (b) Ordinary glass
    (c) Ice
    (d) All

174. Of the following things, which one is made by man?
    (a) Plastics   (b) Petroleum
    (c) Coal   (d) Wood

175. Of the following things, which one can be turned into a magnet?
    (a) Wood piece   (b) Iron piece
    (c) Glass piece   (d) Plastic piece

176. Of the following things, which one is a bad conductor of electricity?
    (a) Copper wire
    (b) Porcelain cup
    (c) Paper clip
    (d) Rupee coin

177. Of the following things, which ones need to be filled with air at great pressure?
    (a) Balloon   (b) Tyre
    (c) Football   (d) Pillow

178. Of the following things, which one does not absorb water?
    (a) Wood   (b) Glass
    (c) Sponge   (d) Wool

179. Of the following things, which one is used as a lever?
    (a) Scissors   (b) Bottle opener
    (c) Screw driver   (d) All

180. Of the following things, which one is not affected by water?
   (a) Rubber   (b) Cotton
   (c) Wool   (d) Wood

181. Of the following things, which one is a biomass?
   (a) Cow dung
   (b) Rotting garbage
   (c) Dead leaves
   (d) All

182. Of the following things, which one needs winds to move?
   (a) Cloud
   (b) Kite
   (c) Pinwheel
   (d) All

183. Of the following things, which one is a good conductor of heat?
   (a) Iron   (b) Plastics
   (c) Glass   (d) Cotton

184. Of the following things, which one does not contain a magnet?
   (a) Electric bell
   (b) Electric motor
   (c) Compass
   (d) Electric torch

185. Of the following things, which one is sold by volume?
   (a) Petrol   (b) Soap
   (c) Chocolate   (d) Rice

186. Of the following things, which one is a bad conductor of heat?
   (a) Air   (b) Glass
   (c) Wood   (d) All

187. Of the following things, which one is not water?
   (a) Tears   (b) Oil
   (c) Dew drops   (d) Sweat

188. Of the following things, which one is a force?
   (a) Height   (b) Area
   (c) Magnetism   (d) Orbit

189. Of the following things, which one is not a product of plants?
   (a) Cloth   (b) Ivory
   (c) Cricket bat   (d) All

190. Of the following things, which one is not made by man?
   (a) Tree
   (b) Socks
   (c) Flowerpot
   (d) Telephone

191. Of the following things, which one does not have either definite shape or size?
    (a) Common salt   (b) Sugar
    (c) Butter   (d) Carbon dioxide

192. Of the following things, which one does not come from an animal?
    (a) Gum   (b) Leather
    (c) Honey   (d) Wool

Sources

193. What is the main source of common salt?
    (a) Plants   (b) Seas
    (c) Rocks   (d) Rains

194. What is the source of plastics?
    (a) Animals   (b) Plants
    (c) Minerals   (d) All

195. What is the source of paper?
    (a) Tree   (b) Animal
    (c) Insect   (d) Rock

196. What are red bricks made of?
    (a) Clay   (b) Cement
    (c) Sand   (d) All

197. What is the source of rubber?
    (a) Animal   (b) Tree
    (c) Bird   (d) Rock

198. What is glass made of?
    (a) Clay   (b) Sandstone
    (c) Pumice   (d) Sand

199. What is the source of coir?
    (a) Jute   (b) Bamboo
    (c) Coconut   (d) Grass

200. What is the source of leather?
    (a) Animal   (b) Insect
    (c) Bird   (d) Tree

201. Of the following things, which one comes
    from an insect?
    (a) Wool   (b) Silk
    (c) Nylon   (d) All

Energy

202. Of the following things, which one is a
    source of heat?
    (a) Clouds   (b) Volcano
    (c) Cyclone   (d) Coral reef

203. What converts electricity into mechanical
    energy?
    (a) Table fan   (b) Refrigerator
    (c) Camera   (d) Invertor

204. Of the following things, which one contains stored energy?
(a) Electric battery (b) Dynamite
(c) Food   (d) All

205. Of the following actions, which one has kinetic energy?
(a) Sea tides
(b) A falling meteor
(c) Water downstream
(d) All

206. Which energy is obtained from the inside of an atom?
(a) Solar energy
(b) Muscular energy
(c) Nuclear energy
(d) Kinetic energy

207. Of the following items, which one runs exclusively on electricity?
(a) Computer
(b) Bicycle
(c) Steam engine
(d) Truck

208. Of the following gadgets, which one converts electricity into heat?
(a) Oven   (b) Tubelight
(c) Telephone   (d) Transistor

209. Which is the natural source of energy?
    (a) Solar energy
    (b) Wind energy
    (c) Geothermal energy
    (d) All

210. Of the following gadgets, which one converts electricity into light?
    (a) Electric bulb
    (b) Toaster
    (c) Microwave oven
    (d) Transistor

211. Of the following actions, which one is the conversion of chemical energy into kinetic energy?
    (a) Pedalling a bicycle
    (b) Driving a motor cycle
    (c) Flying a plane
    (d) All

212. What is energy released by the sun called?
    (a) Cosmic energy
    (b) Fission energy
    (c) Solar energy
    (d) Fusion energy

213. Of the following items, which one does not run or fly on electricity?
    (a) Fan   (b) Aeroplane
    (c) Clock   (d) Motor cycle

214. Of the following natural things, which one has potential energy?
    (a) Glacier on a mountain top
    (b) Hot lava
    (c) Water in a pond
    (d) Morning breeze

215. Which is the most abundant and yet the most primitive source of energy found on the earth?
    (a) Petrol   (b) Coal
    (c) Methane gas   (d) All

216. Of the following things, which one contains kinetic energy?
    (a) Compressed air
    (b) Water tank
    (c) Explosion
    (d) Fuel

217. Of the following gadgets, which one converts electricity into sound?
    (a) Walkman   (b) Stereo system
    (c) Radio   (d) All

218. Of the following natural things, which one can be used for generating electricity?
    (a) Sunlight
    (b) Thunder storm
    (c) Volcano
    (d) Rain

IV

EARTH AND ENVIRONMENT

Earth

219. What is the shape of earth?
    (a) Sphere   (b) Tetrahedron
    (c) Oval   (d) Flat

220. How much time does the earth takes to rotate once about itself?
    (a) 24 hours   (b) 54 hours
    (c) 360 hours   (d) 365 hours

221. Which is the continent that surrounds the south pole?
    (a) Arctic circle   (b) Antarctica
    (c) Eurasia   (d) Australia

222. How many continents are present on the earth?
    (a) Five   (b) Six
    (c) Seven   (d) Eight

223. Where does one find the multi-coloured, dancing lights called "Aurorae"?
    (a) Poles   (b) Equator
    (c) Atlantic Ocean (d) All

224. What percentage of the surface of the earth is land?
    (a) About 27   (b) About 35
    (c) About 42   (d) About 56

225. What emits lava?
    (a) Volcano   (b) Crater
    (c) Lagoon   (d) Island

226. Where are glaciers formed?
    (a) River beds   (b) Mountains
    (c) Oceans   (d) All

227. How many major areas is the ocean on the earth divided into?
    (a) Two   (b) Three
    (c) Four   (d) Five

228. What creates a cave?
    (a) Water   (b) Animal
    (c) Wind   (d) All

229. What covers considerable portion of the earth's surface?
    (a) Petroleum
    (b) Water
    (c) Hydrogen peroxide
    (d) Coal

230. How much time does the earth take to go once around the sun?
    (a) 364 days   (b) 364 ½ days
    (c) 365 days   (d) 365 ¼ days

231. Of the following things, which one is at the centre of the earth?
(a) Magnet
(b) Electric charge
(c) Gases
(d) Hollow sphere

Environment

232. What pollutes rivers?
(a) Sewage   (b) Industries
(c) Garbage   (d) All

233. Of the following things, which one causes most harm to animals, birds and plants?
(a) Vegetable waste
(b) Paper waste
(c) Plastic bags
(d) Clothes

234. Which living beings produce oxygen gas needed by us for breathing?
(a) Birds   (b) Animals
(c) Plants   (d) Trees

235. What causes rotting of dead animals and plants?
(a) Bacteria   (b) Animals
(c) Birds   (d) Trees

236. Which cycle is the most important from the point of living beings?
(a) Water cycle
(b) Carbon cycle
(c) Nitrogen cycle
(d) All

237. Which is the most common plant that grows in all soils?
(a) Grass   (b) Rose
(c) Coconut   (d) Wheat

238. What prevents soil erosion?
(a) Plants   (b) Birds
(c) Earthworms   (d) Animals

239. Where do tides occur?
(a) Seas   (b) Oceans
(c) Lakes   (d) Ponds

240. What do dead bodies of animals and plants form in soil?
(a) Loam   (b) Humus
(c) Manure   (d) Sand

241. What causes floods?
(a) Soil erosion
(b) Heavy rainfall
(c) Forest destruction
(d) All

242. Where do coconut trees grow?
    (a) Mountains
    (b) Plains
    (c) Coast
    (d) Deserts

243. Which is the most poisonous gas released by vehicles?
    (a) Carbon dioxide
    (b) Sulphur dioxide
    (c) Carbon monoxide
    (d) Nitrogen

Weather

244. What causes rains?
    (a) Sun   (b) Clouds
    (c) Moon   (d) Air

245. Of the following events, which one contains electricity?
    (a) Lightning   (b) Thunder
    (c) Rainbow   (d) Fog

246. When is a rainbow seen in the sky?
    (a) Before the rain
    (b) After the rain
    (c) Before sunrise
    (d) After moonrise

247. What causes day and night on the earth?
   (a) Rotation of earth
   (b) Movement of earth
   (c) Stars
   (d) Sun

248. Which is the electrically charged layer in the atmosphere that reflects radio waves?
   (a) Troposphere   (b) Ionosphere
   (c) Stratosphere   (d) Mesosphere

249. When do rains occur more frequently and for days?
   (a) Summer   (b) Winter
   (c) Spring   (d) Monsoon

250. Which gas forms about 78 per cent of the atmosphere?
   (a) Oxygen
   (b) Carbon dioxide
   (c) Nitrogen
   (d) Argon

251. What are clouds made of?
   (a) Chemicals   (b) Water
   (c) Soil   (d) All

252. What is moistness or dampness of air called?
   (a) Fog   (b) Mist
   (c) Humidity   (d) All

253. Of the following things, which one is present in the atmosphere?
(a) Water vapour (b) Dust
(c) Plant spores (d) All

254. What holds the atmosphere to earth?
(a) Gases
(b) Charged particles
(c) Gravity
(d) Vapour pressure

255. What causes thunder?
(a) Moon   (b) Clouds
(c) Sun   (d) Mountains

V

PLANETS, STARS

Planets, Stars, etc.

256. Which is the star that remains fixed in our night sky?
    (a) Rigel
    (b) Alpha Centauri
    (c) Sirius
    (d) Pole star

257. How many planets are present in the solar system?
    (a) Nine   (b) Eleven
    (c) Seven   (d) Thirteen

258. Which heavenly body always keeps the same half facing the earth?
    (a) Moon   (b) Mercury
    (c) Jupiter   (d) Saturn

259. Which planet rotates in a direction opposite to the rest of the planets in the solar system?
    (a) Jupiter   (b) Earth
    (c) Mercury   (d) Venus

260. What causes eclipses?
   (a) Sun   (b) Moon
   (c) Venus   (d) Constellation

261. Which is the planet closest to the Sun in the solar system?
   (a) Mercury   (b) Mars
   (c) Venus   (d) Moon

262. What is not present on the Moon?
   (a) Low gravity   (b) Atmosphere
   (c) Water   (d) Craters

263. When are stars seen in the sky?
   (a) Sunset   (b) Sunrise
   (c) Night   (d) All

264. Which is the most distant planet in the solar system?
   (a) Uranus   (b) Saturn
   (c) Neptune   (d) Pluto

265. What produces a crater on the surface of the Moon?
   (a) A falling body (b) Volcano
   (c) Moonquake   (d) All

266. What is the name of the galaxy in which we live?
    (a) Milky Way
    (b) Andromeda
    (c) Leo A
    (d) NGC 6822

267. Which is the natural satellite of the earth?
    (a) Mercury   (b) Moon
    (c) Venus   (d) Mars

268. In which direction does the sun rise from?
    (a) East   (b) West
    (c) North   (d) South

269. What makes the Moon change its appearance in the sky?
    (a) Sunlight
    (b) Shadow of earth
    (c) Shadow of Moon
    (d) All

270. How many signs is the Zodiac divided into?
    (a) Eight   (b) Nine
    (c) Twelve   (d) Eighteen

271. Which is the largest planet in the solar system?
    (a) Saturn   (b) Jupiter
    (c) Mars   (d) Uranus

272. What are the dark areas on the Moon called?
(a) Mountains   (b) Seas
(c) Volcanoes   (d) Lakes

273. Which planet has a 'Red spot' on its surface?
(a) Venus   (b) Mars
(c) Jupiter   (d) Neptune

274. Which planet is known as the 'morning star' as well as the 'evening star'?
(a) Venus   (b) Saturn
(c) Mars   (d) Mercury

275. Of the following constellations, which one represents a lion?
(a) Gemini   (b) Leo
(c) Cancer   (d) Taurus

VI

MATTER, FORCES, SHAPES

Matter, Forces, etc.

276. How many colours are seen in the spectrum of white light?
    (a) Five   (b) Seven
    (c) Nine   (d) Ten

277. Which force is commonly and uniformly applied to all bodies on earth?
    (a) Friction
    (b) Gravity
    (c) Electric force
    (d) Magnetic force

278. Where does the "siphon" action take place?
    (a) Water supply to homes
    (b) Fountain
    (c) Drinking cola with a straw
    (d) All

279. How many poles does a magnet have?
    (a) One   (b) Two
    (c) Three   (d) Four

280. How many kinds of solids are present in nature?
(a) Two　　　　　(b) Three
(c) Four　　　　　(d) Five

281. When a body is floating in say, water, what force does it experience in the upward direction?
(a) Gravity　　　(b) Buoyancy
(c) Magnetic force (d) Inertia

282. What requires force to do the work?
(a) Pedalling a bicycle
(b) Flying a kite
(c) Squeezing a toothpaste
(d) All

283. Which is a form of energy?
(a) Electricity　　(b) Heat
(c) Matter　　　　(d) All

284. What expands a metal?
(a) Electricity　　(b) Heat
(c) Light　　　　　(d) All

285. How many states of matter exist?
(a) Three　　　　(b) Four
(c) Five　　　　　(d) Six

286. What makes water always run downhill?
(a) Gravity　　　(b) Pressure
(c) Friction　　　(d) All

287. Which force resists the motion of two bodies against each other?
(a) Inertia   (b) Viscosity
(c) Friction   (d) Gravity

288. What is the process that converts a solid into its vapours?
(a) Evaporisation   (b) Condensation
(c) Sublimation   (d) All

289. What cannot be created or destroyed?
(a) Energy   (b) Matter
(c) Both   (d) None

290. Which state of matter has no fixed shape or volume?
(a) Solid   (b) Liquid
(c) Gas   (d) All

291. Where does friction come into play?
(a) Pushing a box
(b) Opening a door
(c) Cleaning a utensil
(d) All

292. What changes liquid into gas?
(a) Condensation   (b) Convection
(b) Evaporation   (d) All

293. When does melting take place?
(a) Ice turns to water
(b) Iron becomes red

(c) Water droplets are formed

(d) Milk turns into ice cream

294. What is a 'pulley' used for?
    (a) Lifting heavy loads
    (b) Rolling a cask up
    (c) Holding an ice cube
    (d) Changing the direction of rotation of a wheel

295. How many types of electric charges are there?
    (a) One   (b) Two
    (c) Three   (d) Four

Shapes and Figures

296. Of the following things, which one is associated with a circle?
    (a) Centre   (b) Diametre
    (c) Circumference (d) All

297. What is the shape of a sugar crystal?
    (a) Cube   (b) Cylinder
    (c) Cuboid   (d) Pyramid

298. Of the following gadgets, which one shows angles?
    (a) Wall clock   (b) Water tap
    (c) Gas cooker   (d) Television

299. What is the shape of a brick?
    (a) Cube   (b) Cuboid
    (c) Sphere   (d) Tetrahedron

300. Of the following figures, which one is called 'a fraction of 7'?
    (a) 7.0   (b) 0.7
    (c) 0.07   (d) 1/7

301. What is the shape of this Egyptian monument?
    (a) Pyramid
    (b) Cylinder
    (c) Tetrahedron
    (d) Circle

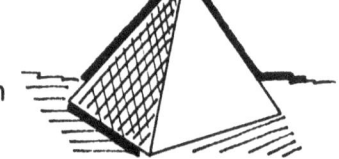

302. Of the following figures, which one is called 'square of 4':
    (a) 4 x 2   (b) 4 x 3
    (c) 4 x 4   (d) 4 x 5

303. What is the shape of a pencil?
    (a) Cone   (b) Cylinder
    (c) Hexagon   (d) Sphere

304. Of the following expressions, which one is called 'cube of six':
    (a) 3 x 6
    (b) 6 x 6 x 6 x 6
    (c) 6 x 6 x 6
    (d) 6 x 3 x 3

305. What is the usual shape of a birthday cap?
    (a) Square   (b) Cone
    (c) Pyramid   (d) Cube

306. What is the shape of the Moon?
    (a) Triangle   (b) Circle
    (c) Rectangle   (d) Square

307. What would railway lines be called?
    (a) Perpendicular lines
    (b) Acute angles
    (c) Parallel lines
    (d) Chord

308. Of the following figures, which one is called 'a multiple of 8'?
    (a) 24   (b) 25
    (c) 26   (d) 27

309. What is the shape of a cable television aerial?
    (a) Sphere
    (b) Hexagon
    (c) Tetrahedron
    (d) Hemisphere

310. Of the following figures, which one is called 'a divisor of 27'?
    (a) 4   (b) 7
    (c) 9   (d) 11

311. What is the shape of a kite?
   (a) Rectangle   (b) Ellipse
   (c) Square   (d) Cube

312. Of the following figures, which one has '8 as denominator'?
   (a) 6/8   (b) 7/8
   (c) 1/8   (d) All

313. What is the shape of a football ground?
   (a) Trapezium   (b) Circle
   (c) Rectangle   (d) Cone

314. What does ÷ represent?
   (a) Multiplication (b) Addition
   (c) Subtraction   (d) Division

315. What is 1,000?
   (a) One hundred   (b) One thousand
   (c) Ten   (d) Ten thousand

316. What is the shape of a ball?
   (a) Sphere   (b) Cube
   (c) Tetrahedron   (d) Cuboid

Chemicals, Gases, etc.

317. Which gas supports a candle flame?
   (a) Oxygen   (b) Nitrogen
   (c) Carbon dioxide (d) Hydrogen

318. Of the following substances, which one is not a compound?
(a) Water   (b) Common salt
(c) Carbon dioxide (d) Iron

319. Which process is used to clean water?
(a) Decantation   (b) Sedimentation
(b) Filteration   (d) All

320. How much oxygen is present in the air?
(a) 11 per cent
(b) 21 per cent
(c) 34 per cent
(d) 48 per cent

321. Which metal is the best conductor of electricity?
(a) Silver   (b) Gold
(c) Copper   (d) Bismuth

322. What does an acid taste like?
(a) Bitter   (b) Sour
(c) Sweet   (d) Salty

323. Which gas is present in all fizzy or soft drinks?
(a) Nitrogen   (b) Carbon dioxide
(c) Ammonia   (d) Chlorine

324. What does a diamond contain?
(a) Sodium   (b) Carbon
(c) Iron   (d) Sulphur

325. Of the following metals, which is often used for electrical wiring?
(a) Copper
(b) Steel
(c) Silver
(d) Bronze

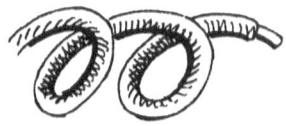

326. Which is a fossil fuel?
(a) Coal
(b) Petrol
(c) Natural gas
(d) All

327. What is a candle made of?
(a) Paraffin wax
(b) Camphor
(c) Plastics
(d) Wood

328. Which gas is used for cooking purposes?
(a) Methane
(b) Helium
(c) Oxygen
(d) Ammonia

329. What is the 'lead' in pencils?
(a) Silver
(b) Carbon
(c) Lead
(d) All

VII

TOOLS, COMPUTER, DEVICES

Computers

330. Where does anything fed into the computer seen?
     (a) Monitor   (b) C.P.U.
     (c) Printer   (d) Keyboard

331. Of the following things, which one is not fixed to a computer?
     (a) Floppy disk   (b) Hard disk
     (c) Monitor   (d) Keyboard

332. Of the following parts of a computer, which one looks like a TV screen?
     (a) Monitor   (b) Keyboard
     (c) Printer   (d) Mouse

333. Where is the 'cursor' seen in a computer?
     (a) Keyboard   (b) Monitor
     (c) Printer   (d) Hard disk

334. Where is the 'motherboard' — the main electronic circuit board — located in a computer?
     (a) System unit   (b) Keyboard
     (c) Printer   (d) Mouse

335. Which is the longest key in the keyboard of a computer?
(a) Shift   (b) Enter
(c) Space bar   (d) Caps lock

336. Which is the key to be pressed to reset a computer?
(a) Ctrl   (b) Alt
(c) Del   (d) All

337. What is the 'brain' of a computer?
(a) Memory   (b) Keyboard
(c) Silicon chip   (d) Printer

338. What is used for connecting a computer to the internet?
(a) MODEM   (b) CD-ROM
(c) Mouse   (d) Scanner

339. What should a computer have, if one wants to use it for multimedia applications?
(a) Speakers
(b) CD-ROM drive
(c) Microphone
(d) All

Tools, Devices and Instruments

340. What is this device used for?
    (a) Weather
    (b) Star position
    (c) Wind direction
    (d) Sun position

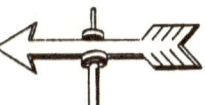

341. What is this tool used for?
    (a) Measuring breadth
    (b) Measuring length
    (c) Measuring diameter
    (d) All

342. What is used for seeing distant objects so that they can be studied in detail?
    (a) Telescope   (b) Kaleidoscope
    (c) Periscope   (d) Stethoscope

343. What is this tool used for?
    (A) Radius
    (b) Length
    (c) Width
    (d) All

344. What is used to measure atmospheric pressure?
    (a) Barometer
    (b) Manometer
    (c) Thermometer
    (d) All

345. What is this gadget used for?
   (a) Length
   (b) Time
   (c) Weight
   (d) Temperature

346. What is this device used for measuring?
   (a) Length
   (b) Diameter
   (c) Angle
   (d) Radius

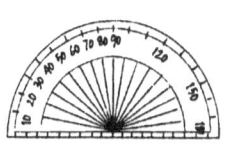

347. What is used to measure blood pressure in a human body?
   (a) Stethoscope
   (b) Microscope
   (c) Sphygmomanometer
   (d) Barometer

348. What is this instrument used for?
   (a) Examining Heart beats
   (b) Examining nose
   (c) Examining ears
   (d) Examining stomach

349. Which instrument magnifies the size of a nearby object so that it can be studied in detail?
(a) Periscope   (b) Spectroscope
(c) Telescope   (d) Microscope

350. What does this instrument measure?
(a) Rainfall
(b) Air pressure
(c) Wind direction
(d) River level

351. What is a thermometer used for?
(a) Measuring temperature of a body
(b) Measuring height of a body
(c) Measuring diameter of a body
(d) Measuring blood in a body

352. What is used for checking whether a wall is perpendicular and straight?
(a) Plumb line   (b) Sextant
(c) Divider   (d) Sundial

353. What is this instrument used for?
(a) Drawing a circle
(b) Drawing a square
(c) Drawing parallel lines
(d) Drawing a triangle

354. What is this device used for measuring?
   (a) Mass
   (b) Length
   (c) Density
   (d) All

355. Which instrument is used for finding out directions?
   (a) Watch
   (b) Magnetic compass
   (c) Wind vane
   (d) Voltmeter

VIII

SUBJECT AND PROFESSION

Subjects

356. What is the study of energy and matter called?
    (a) Physics   (b) Astronomy
    (c) Chemistry   (d) Biology

357. What is the study of plants called?
    (a) Botany   (b) Zoology
    (c) Biology   (d) Geology

358. Which subject deals with shapes, lines and measurements?
    (a) Arithmetic
    (b) Geometry
    (c) Algebra
    (d) Statistics

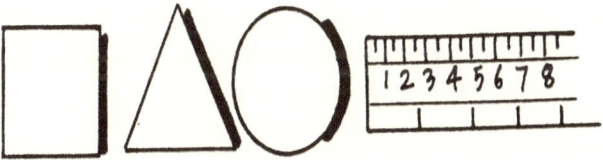

359. What is the study of elements and their compounds, and the reactions they undergo?
    (a) Chemistry   (b) Physics
    (c) Biochemistry   (d) Biotechnology

360. What is the science of living beings called?
    (a) Biotechnology   (b) Biology
    (c) Zoology   (d) Botany

361. What is the study of oceans called?
    (a) Oceanography   (b) Paleontology
    (c) Geology   (d) Hydrology

362. Which subject deals with the physical features of the earth, climate, population and products?
    (a) Geology   (b) Climatology
    (c) Geography   (d) Physics

363. What is the study of atmosphere called?
    (a) Geology   (b) Meteorology
    (c) Atmosphere   (d) Climatology

364. What is the study of earth called?
    (a) Geology   (b) Geography
    (c) Paleontology   (d) Zoology

365. What does biology consist of?
    (a) Zoology and botany
    (b) Geology and zoology
    (c) Geology and botany
    (d) Geology and chemistry

366. What is the study of stars, planets and other heavenly bodies called?
(a) Cosmology   (b) Astronomy
(c) Geology   (d) Zoology

Professions

367. Who examines the human body, inquires about symptoms and gives medicines?
(a) Doctor   (b) Engineer
(c) Surgeon   (d) Mechanic

368. Who builds structures, such as, houses, bridges, dams, etc.?
(a) Engineer   (b) Contractor
(c) Architect   (d) Physicist

369. Who repairs cars, scooters, aeroplanes, etc.?
(a) Mechanic   (b) Engineer
(c) Plumber   (d) Chemist

370. Who prepares medicines and gives injections in a doctor's clinic?
    (a) Technician
    (b) Laboratory assistant
    (c) Compounder
    (d) All

371. Who repairs house wiring and electrical gadgets?
    (a) Mechanic   (b) Technician
    (c) Electrician   (d) Foreman

372. Who studies the night sky and heavenly bodies?
    (a) Astrologer   (b) Meteorologist
    (c) Cosmologist   (d) Astronomer

373. Who performs surgical operations?
    (a) Geologist   (b) Zoologist
    (c) Surgeon   (d) Dietician

374. Who studies about nature in a laboratory?
    (a) Scientist   (b) Technologist
    (c) Engineer   (d) Inventor

375. Who enters and works in the outer space?
    (a) Astronaut   (b) Cosmonaut
    (c) Cosmologist   (d) Astronomer

376. Who assists a doctor in the treatment of an ill person?
    (a) Compounder   (b) Nurse
    (c) Technician   (d) Mechanic

IX

FIRSTS AND RECORDS

Firsts

377. Who is the first person to travel in space?
    (a) Michael Collins (b) Yuri Gargarin
    (c) John Glenn   (d) Neil Armstrong

378. Which is the first space ferry?
    (a) *Skylab*   (b) Space Shuttle
    (c) *Soyuz - 4*   (d) Spacelab

379. Who is the first Indian astronaut?
    (a) Ravish Malhotra
    (b) Rakesh Sharma
    (c) Radhakrishnan
    (d) Kalpana Chawla

380. Who is the first man to step on the Moon?
    (a) John Glenn
    (b) Michael Collins
    (c) Neil Armstrong
    (d) Yuri Gargarin

381. Which is the first spacecraft to go into
    orbit of the earth?
    (a) *Vostok - 1*   (b) *Apollo - 1*
    (c) *Sputnik - 1*   (d) *Geo - 1*

382. Who is the first person to claim that the earth is round and that it rotates?
(a) Nicolaus Copernicus
(b) Aryabhatta
(c) Aristotle
(d) Johannes Kepler

383. Which is the first space station?
(a) *Skylab*   (b) *Salyut - 1*
(c) *Space lab*   (d) *Salyut - 6*

384. Who is the first person to reach the South Pole?
(a) Robert E. Peary
(b) Marco Polo
(c) Roald Amundsen
(d) James Cook

385. Which is the first planet to be discovered in the modern times?
(a) Jupiter   (b) Uranus
(c) Neptune   (d) Mercury

386. Which is India's first satellite to go into space?
(a) *Rohini - 2*   (b) *Aryabhatta*
(c) APPLE   (d) INSAT - 2B

387. Who is the first woman to enter space?
(a) Valentina Tereshkova
(b) Sally Ride
(c) Kalpana Chawla
(d) Mary Cleave

388. Which is the first city where an atom bomb was dropped?
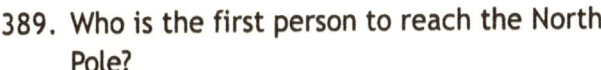
(a) Hiroshima
(b) Nagasaki
(c) Osaka
(d) Tokyo

389. Who is the first person to reach the North Pole?
(a) Robert Falcon Scott
(b) Ronald Amundsen
(c) Robert Peary
(d) Ernest Shackleton

390. Who was the first explorer to travel once around the earth?
(a) Francis Drake
(b) Christopher Columbus
(c) Marco Polo
(d) James Cook

391. Who is the first Indian woman astronaut to go into space?
(a) Kalpana Sharma
(b) Kalpana Chawla
(c) Juhi Chawla
(d) Padmini Iyer

Records

392. Which is the largest bird alive today?
     (a) Emu   (b) Ostrich
     (c) Peacock   (d) Black patridge

393. Which is the deepest ocean?
     (a) Pacific ocean
     (b) Indian ocean
     (c) Atlantic ocean
     (d) Arctic ocean

394. Which is the largest desert in the world?
     (a) Gobi desert   (b) Sahara desert
     (c) Thar desert   (d) Negev desert

395. Which is the largest country in the world?
     (a) Canada   (b) Russia
     (c) USA   (d) China

396. Which is the highest mountain system in the world?
     (a) Alps   (b) Urals
     (c) Himalayas   (d) Andes

397. Which is the smallest bird alive today?
     (a) Little flowerpecker
     (b) Bee hummingbird
     (c) Kiwi
     (d) White wagtail

398. Which is the largest continent in the world?
(a) Asia
(b) Antarctica
(c) South America
(d) North America

399. Which is the largest island in the world?
(a) Greenland   (b) Borneo
(c) Sri Lanka   (d) Australia

400. Which is the largest animal that has ever lived on the earth?
(a) Rhinoceros
(b) Blue whale
(c) Elephant
(d) Brontosaurus

401. Which is the highest peak in the world?
(a) Kilimanjaro
(b) Mount Erebus
(c) Mount Everest
(d) Makalu

402. Which is the largest ocean in the world?
   (a) Atlantic ocean
   (b) Pacific ocean
   (c) Indian ocean
   (d) Arctic ocean

403. Which is the most intelligent fish?
   (A) Eel   (b) Dolphin
   (c) Shark   (d) Whale

X

MISCELLANEOUS

Miscellaneous

404. Which is the standard scale for measuring the temperature of a body?
    (a) Celsius   (b) Centigrade
    (c) Fahrenheit   (d) Reaumer

405. What is Taj Mahal made of?
    (a) Obsidian   (b) Limestone
    (c) Marble   (d) Gneiss

406. Where is vacuum present in nature?
    (a) Plant   (b) Soil
    (c) Space   (d) Earth

407. Which is the longest day of the year?
    (a) 21 January
    (b) 21 November
    (c) 21 April
    (d) 21 June

408. What is the standard unit for measuring milk?
    (a) Litre   (b) Pint
    (c) Gallon   (d) All

409. Which grass is the main food of more than half the population of the world?
    (a) Rice   (b) Wheat
    (c) Bamboo   (d) Rye

410. What is Red Fort made up of?
    (a) Sandstone
    (b) Granite
    (c) Limestone
    (d) Pumice

411. What is the temperature at which water boils?
    (a) 10^0 Celsius
    (b) 100^0 Celsius
    (c) 1000^0 Celsius
    (d) 10000^0 Celsius

412. What is the standard unit for measuring cloth?
    (a) Foot   (b) Yard
    (c) Metre   (d) Centimetre

413. When is the National Science Day celebrated in India every year?
    (a) 26 January
    (b) 15 August
    (c) 28 February
    (d) 5 June

414. What is the normal temperature of the human body?
    (a) About 90^0
    (b) About 92^0
    (c) About 98^0
    (d) About 100^0

415. What is the standard unit for measuring one's weight?
    (a) Pound   (b) Metre
    (c) Kilogram   (d) Litre

XI

PORTRAIT QUIZ

Identify these famous scientists or inventors and mention their discoveries or inventions.

416.

417.

418.

419.

420.

421.

422.

423.

424.

425.

ANSWERS

1. (a)	2. (d)	3. (d)	4. (c)
5. (a)	6. (b)	7. (a)	8. (b)
9. (a)	10. (d)	11. (c)	12. (a)
13. (d)	14. (a)	15. (b)	16. (a)
17. (a) and (b)	18.(a)	19. (d)	20. (b)
21. (b)	22. (a)	23. (b)	24. (b)
25. (a)	26. (a)	27. (a)	28. (c)
29. (c)	30. (b)	31. (a)	32. (a)
33. (b)	34. (b)	35. (c)	36. (a)
37. (a)	38. (d)	39. (c)	40. (c)
41. (a)	42. (a)	43. (d)	44. (a)
45. (a)	46. (c)	47. (b)	48. (a)
49. (b)	50. (b)	51. (b)	
52. (b) and (d)		53. (a)	54. (c)
55. (b)	56. (a)	57. (b)	58. (c)
59. (d)	60. (b)	61. (b)	62. (c)
63. (d)	64. (a)	65. (a)	66. (c)
67. (d)	68. (d)	69. (b)	70. (a)
71. (c)	72. (c)	73. (a)	74. (b)
75. (a) It hops — not flies.			
76. (a) and (c)		77. (d)	78. (c)
79. (a)	80. (c)	81. (b)	82. (d)
83. (a)	84. (a)	85. (b)	86. (c)
87. (d)	88. (d)	89. (c)	90. (a)
91. (c) and (d)		92. (b)	93. (d)
94. (a)			
95. (a) Minute holes in the leaves called stomata			
96. (c)	97. (b)		

98. (d) Plants need water and   sunlight   to
    produce food.
99. (c)   100. (b)   101. (c)   102. (b)
103. (c)   104. (d)   105. (b)   106. (c)
107. (d)   108. (b)
109. (b) Incisors, canines, premolars and molars.
110. (d)   111. (c)   112. (c)   113. (c)
114. (b)   115. (b)   116. (a)   117. (d)
118. (b)   119. (b)   120. (d)   121. (d)
122. (b)   123. (a)   124. (b)   125. (a)
126. (d)   127. (d)   128. (a)   129. (a)
130. (d)   131. (a)   132. (c)   133. (b)
134. (b)   135. (d)   136. (a)   137. (c)
138. (d)   139. (b)   140. (b)   141. (c)
142. (c)   143. (b)   144. (c)   145. (c)
146. (a)   147. (d)   148. (d)   149. (d)
150. (a)   151. (c)   152. (d)   153. (c)
154. (c)   155. (b)   156. (b)   157. (c)
158. (a)   159. (c)
160. (b) Some colours are invisible
161. (c)   162. (b)   163. (c)   164. (a)
165. (c)   166. (a)   167. (d)   168. (d)
169. (d)   170. (d)   171. (b)   172. (a)
173. (d)   174. (a)   175. (b)   176. (b)
177. (b) and (c)   178. (b)   179. (d)
180. (a)   181. (d)   182. (d)   183. (a)
184. (d)   185. (a)   186. (d)   187. (b)
188. (c)   189. (b)   190. (a)   191. (d)
192. (a)   193. (b)   194. (c)   195. (a)
196. (a)   197. (b)   198. (d)   199. (c)
200. (a)   201. (b)   202. (b)   203. (a)

204. (d)   205. (d)   206. (c)   207. (a)
208. (a)   209. (d)   210. (a)   211. (d)
212. (c)   213. (b)   214. (a)   215. (b)
216. (c)   217. (d)   218. (a)
219. (a) To be precise, oblate spheroid.
220. (a)   221. (b)   222. (c)   223. (a)
224. (b)   225. (a)   226. (b)
227. (c) Pacific, Atlantic, Indian and Arctic.
228. (a) Flow of water slowly erodes rocks and
         forms caves.
229. (b)   230. (d)
231. (a)   232. (d)   233. (c)
234. (c) and (d)
235. (a)   236. (d)   237. (a)   238. (a)
239. (a)   240. (b)   241. (d)   242. (c)
243. (c)   244. (b)   245. (a)   246. (b)
247. (a)   248. (b)   249. (d)   250. (c)
251. (b)   252. (c)   253. (d)   254. (c)
255. (b)   256. (d)   257. (a)   258. (a)
259. (d)   260. (a) and (b)   261. (a)
262. (b) Recent studies show water on the Moon
263. (d)   264. (d)   265. (a)   266. (a)
267. (b)   268. (a)   269. (a)
270. (c)   271. (b)
272. (b) Called "Maria" in Latin.
273. (c)   274. (a)   275. (b)   276. (b)
277. (b)   278. (d)
279. (b) South and North poles.
280. (a) Crystal and Non-crystal or amorphous.
281. (b)   282. (d)   283. (d)   284. (b)

285. (b) Solid, liquid, gaseous and plasma. Often, the last is not commonly known.

286. (a)   287. (c)   288. (c)   289. (c)

290. (c)   291. (d)   292. (c)   293. (a)

294. (a)   295. (b)   296. (d)   297. (a)

298. (a) Needles are often at angles.

299. (b)   300. (d)   301. (a)   302. (c)

303. (b)   304. (c)   305. (b)   306. (b)

307. (c)   308. (a)   309. (d)   310. (c)

311. (c) To be exact, Quadrilateral.

312. (d)   313. (c)   314. (d)   315. (b)

316. (a)   317. (a)   318. (d)   319. (d)

320. (b)   321. (a)   322. (b)   323. (b)

324. (b)   325. (a)   326. (d)   327. (a)

328. (a)

329. (b) A form of carbon called "Graphite".

330. (a)   331. (a)   332. (a)   333. (b)

334. (a)   335. (c)   336. (d)   337. (c)

338. (a)   339. (d)   340. (c)   341. (d)

342. (a)   343. (d)   344. (a)   345. (b)

346. (c)   347. (c)   348. (a)   349. (d)

350. (a)   351. (a)   352. (a)   353. (a)

354. (a)   355. (b)   356. (a)   357. (a)

358. (b)   359. (a)   360. (b)   361. (a)

362. (c)   363. (b)   364. (a)   365. (a)

366. (b)   367. (a)   368. (a)   369. (a)

370. (c)   371. (c)   372. (d)   373. (c)

374. (a)   375. (a) and (b)   376. (b)

377. (b)   378. (b)   379. (b)   380. (c)

381. (c) Launched by the Russians in 1957.

382. (b)

383. (b) It was launched in 1971 by Russia.
384. (c)   385. (b)   386. (b)
387. (a) A Russian cosmonaut.
388. (a)   389. (c)   390. (a)
391. (b) She is now an American citizen.
392. (b)   393. (a)   394. (b)   395. (b)
396. (c)   397. (b)   398. (a)
399. (a) Australia is usually considered to be a continent not an island.
400. (b)   401. (c)   402. (b)   403. (b)
404. (a)   405. (c)   406. (c)   407. (d)
408. (a)   409. (a)   410. (a)   411. (b)
412. (c)   413. (c)   414. (c)   415. (c)
416. Marie Curie and radium.
417. Thomas Edison and electric bulb.
418. Isaac Newton and the law of gravitation.
419. Galileo Gálilei and the laws of falling bodies.
420. Willam Harvey and the circulation of blood.
421. John Baird and the television.
422. Charles Babbage and computer.
423. J. C. Bose and the radio.
424. Albert Einstein and the mass energy formula.
425. C. V. Raman and the Raman Effect.

SCORE YOURSELF!

Count the correct answers you
have given and mark
yourself as follows:
Average: if 256 answers are correct
Good: if 298 answers are correct
Excellent: if 340 answers are correct
And if you score more than 385 correct
You're a SUPERKID in science!